STO

FRIENDS
OF ACPL

BOOKS BY SCOTT CORBETT

The Trick Books

The Lemonade Trick
The Mailbox Trick
The Disappearing Dog Trick
The Baseball Trick
The Turnabout Trick
The Hairy Horror Trick
The Home Run Trick
The Hockey Trick
The Black Mask Trick
The Hangman's Ghost Trick

Suspense Stories

Cop's Kid
Tree House Island
Dead Man's Light
Cutlass Island
One by Sea
The Baseball Bargain
The Mystery Man
Dead Before Docking
Run for the Money
The Case of the Gone Goose
The Case of the Fugitive Firebug
The Case of the Ticklish Tooth
The Case of the Silver Skull
The Case of the Burgled Blessing Box

Easy-to-Read Adventures

Dr. Merlin's Magic Shop
The Great Custard Pie Panic
The Boy Who Walked on Air
The Foolish Dinosaur Fiasco
The Mysterious Zetabet
The Great McGoniggle's Gray Ghost
The Great McGoniggle's Key Play
The Great McGoniggle Rides Shotgun
The Great McGoniggle Switches Pitches

What Makes It Work?

What Makes a Car Go?
What Makes TV Work?
What Makes a Light Go On?
What Makes a Plane Fly?
What Makes a Boat Float?

Ghost Stories

The Red Room Riddle
Here Lies the Body
Captain Butcher's Body

Nonfiction for Older Readers

Home Computers: A Simple and
   Informative Guide

The Great McGoniggle Switches Pitches

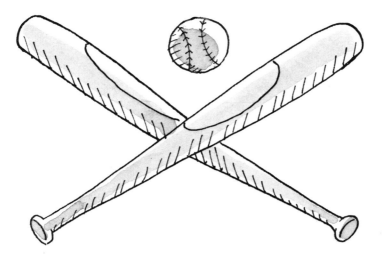

the Great McGoniggle Switches Pitches

by SCOTT CORBETT

Illustrated by Bill Ogden

An Atlantic Monthly Press Book
Little, Brown and Company

Boston   Toronto

TEXT COPYRIGHT © 1980 BY SCOTT CORBETT
ILLUSTRATIONS COPYRIGHT © 1980 BY WILLIAM OGDEN

FIRST EDITION

Library of Congress Cataloging in Publication Data

Corbett, Scott.
    The Great McGoniggle switches pitches.

    An Atlantic Monthly Press book.
    SUMMARY: With Kilroy High's victory hanging in
the balance, Mac McGoniggle calls a surprising pitch
in the championship game against Gunther High.
    [1. Baseball — Fiction] I. Ogden, William, fl.
1972–   II. Title.
PZ7.C79938Go [Fic]   80–15589
ISBN 0–316–15710–4

ATLANTIC–LITTLE, BROWN BOOKS
ARE PUBLISHED BY
LITTLE, BROWN AND COMPANY
IN ASSOCIATION WITH
THE ATLANTIC MONTHLY PRESS

BP

Published simultaneously in Canada
by Little, Brown & Company (Canada) Limited

PRINTED IN THE UNITED STATES OF AMERICA

To Mary and Ed Safford,
who love baseball as much as I do

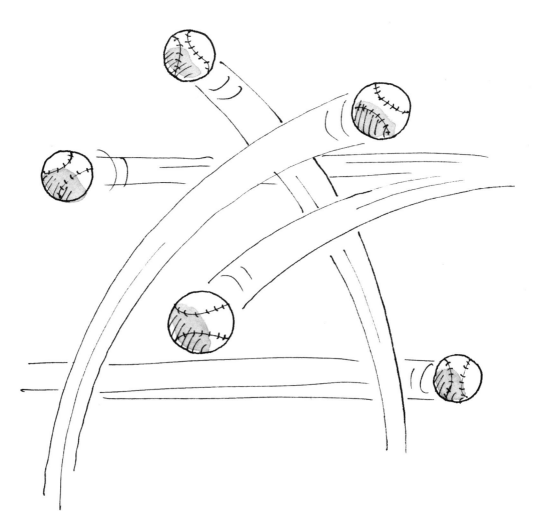

1

"KEN, your fast ball is humming! And your change-up pitch is going to tie them in knots." Mac McGoniggle crouched down again and pounded the pocket of his catcher's mitt. "Now all we need is a batter!"

Ken Wetzel and Mac stopped to watch the game from the bullpen. Bottom of the eighth. Their team, Kilroy High, leading 7–2. Their superstar, Chad Watson, had gone three for four at the plate. Mac sighed.

"If I spend much more time here in the bullpen I'll grow horns and a tail," he said. "Wouldn't it be my luck to land on a team where the best hitter is the catcher?"

"I thought up a poem about that," said Ken.

"The Great McGoniggle's swing is quaint;
As a hitter, great he ain't!"

"It has come to my attention that our splendid first-string pitcher, Mr. Amato, is also having a good day," retorted Mac.

"I noticed that. At the rate Motty's mowing them down I'll *never* get to pitch!"

The outlook from the bullpen was bleak.

"We're surprising the whole league!" Coach Coogan surveyed his squad with an old drill-sergeant's glare of approval. "Four straight wins and three to go! We're gonna keep winning and Kilroy's gonna take Gunther High no matter *how* many sets of fireballing, fence-busting twins a certain coach steals from us!"

Gunther's Coach Hammond was a sore point with Coogan. When Kilroy was upgraded to a four-year high, the Simmons twins should have gone to Kilroy, but somehow they ended up enrolled at Gunther.

"But don't forget," Coach added grimly, "we can't afford to lose *any* games, not one game, if we want to beat out Gunther, because I don't see Gunther losing to anyone but us. So we've got to take them all."

Chad Watson flashed a wide grin.

"Don't worry, Coach, we will. And we're going to pulverize Gunther!"

"How to you spell that, Chad?" someone yelled.

"W-I-N," said Chad. "We're going to finish the season *and* Gunther all at once!"

2

KILROY'S FIFTH GAME was a home game with Finley High. After Friday practice Coach Coogan called Ken and Mac aside.

"Finley ought to be a breeze. I shouldn't need you guys, so I'm giving you a special detail. Gunther's playing Hawthorne at home. I want you to scout Gunther's team, especially those Simmons twins. Bring back all the dope you can. Take your bikes and sit in the third-base stands near the outfield end.

If I see any signs of trouble I'll send someone on the double to get you."

"So now we're scouts," complained Ken as they pedaled over to Gunther High Saturday

morning. "Next thing you know we'll be scorekeepers!"

But Mac was making the best of things. He usually did.

"Scouts? Mere scouts? Don't talk about scouts! This is dangerous business. Secret agents is more like it. Why do you think I wore my dark glasses? If Gunther's counter-spies find out who we are, our lives won't be worth a nickel!"

The Great McGoniggle looked so funny hunched low over the handlebars, shooting wary glances in all directions, that Ken stopped grumbling and laughed.

They chained their bikes alongside the school building and walked over to the field. The game provided no surprises, with the big, rawboned Simmons twins living up to

their advance billing. They were a battery —
Frank pitched, Ernie caught. Both were as
good as advertised. Frank couldn't hit, but
Ernie made up for him in that department.

"How do you like their names — Frank
and Ernest! Their father must be quite a jok-
er," said Mac. "You know what, Ken? Frank
reminds me of you."

"Me? How?"

"He's a southpaw."

"Yeah, and that's about it. He's out of my
league."

"He hasn't got as good a change-up as you
have."

"He doesn't need it."

"It's interesting, though. He's a lefty, and
Ernie's right-handed. You'd think identical
twins would be alike in everything."

Then suddenly a pair of arms was wind-
milling down beside the stands, and Tommy
Lutz was yelling, "Mac! Ken!"

"Hey! We must be needed! Let's go!"

3

"MOTTY hasn't got his stuff today!" Tommy shouted as they pedaled madly back to Kilroy. "He's walking guys like crazy! When I left, our lead was down to three!"

The locker room had never seen uniforms fly on so fast. The scoreboard gave them the bad news — Finley had a one-run lead! Kilroy was at bat in the bottom of the eighth, with men on.

"What kept you?" yelled Coach Coogan.

"Start warming up — I may need you!"

"This is terrible!" said Ken. "You know what Coach said — we can't afford to lose a single game. And from the way Gunther looked today, he's right."

"Then we'll just have to pull this one out," said Mac. And when Chad drove in two runs with a triple, Mac yelled, "This is your lucky day, Ken! There's your lead!"

"Huh! Motty will probably hold them now!"

"I don't wish him any bad luck," said Mac, "but keep warming up!"

In the top of the ninth the first batter popped up on a bad pitch. But then Motty walked the next two.

Coach Coogan waved to the bullpen.

13

"Mac! Look! Coach is — is —"

"Man of Destiny, your hour has come — Hey, wait for me!"

Coach had news. "Mac, you know how to handle Ken, so we're moving Chad to first base and you're catching."

The close-set eyes of the Great McGoniggle did pinwheel turns.

"Me, too? Wow!"

Ken went to the mound, replacing an unhappy Motty. While Chad was transferring the catcher's chest protector and shin guards to Mac, Ken threw warm-up pitches to Tommy. His first pitch went over Tommy's head, drawing hoots from Finley rooters, but after that he zeroed in. Mac was ready in time to take Ken's last two warm-up tosses. They were right in the groove. Mac trotted to the mound.

14

"Give this next guy fast balls low and on the corners. Let's go — all we need is two outs!"

15

Ken wanted to say, "Sure, and all Napoleon needed was to win at Waterloo!" but he didn't. Two outs!

When the left-handed batter stepped in, Ken set himself, gave the runner on second a hard look over his shoulder, and threw his first pitch.

Crack!

A late swing sent the ball straight down the first base line into the mitt of Chad Watson, who stepped on the bag to double the runner for the third out before he could get back to the base. The game was over.

When they came out of the gym after showering and dressing, most of the crowd had gone, but a dapper little man was leaning against the building, enjoying a slim cigar.

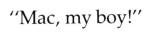

"Mac, my boy!"

Mac looked surprised and pleased. "Uncle Shamus! What are you doing here?"

"What do you mean, lad — I saw the whole game, and a grand game it was, especially that last pitch, which was thrown by this fine young fellow here, if I'm not mistaken?"

"Right! Uncle Shamus, meet Ken Wetzel."

Ken looked into twinkling blue McGoniggle eyes much like Mac's.

"We weren't at our best today, Uncle Shamus," Mac went on. "At least, Motty wasn't."

"I'm glad to hear that. I was talking only the other night to a friend whose grandsons are at Gunther High, and he claims Gunther's the whole show. You'll be playing them soon, I hear. And how do you expect to do?"

"We'll mop them up!"

"That's what I like to hear! And how do you see it, Ken?"

"With Motty working right and a hitter like Chad in the lineup, we can't miss!"

Uncle Shamus beamed his approval. "Splendid, splendid! I wish my big blow-hard friend Colin Simmons could hear you; it would send a chill down his spine!"

"Who?"

"Colin Simmons. I couldn't stand his boasting, so I bet him fifty dollars my nephew and Kilroy would win!"

"What?" Mac's clown face did a quick change from comedy to tragedy. "Uncle Shamus, are you crazy?"

"Crazy? Now, what kind of talk is that from a McGoniggle? Not a moment ago you said . . ."

"But — but that was just pep talk, and — Simmons! Are his grandsons the twins, Frank and Ernie?"

"The very ones, and did you ever hear such ridiculous names —"

"Never mind their names, they're dynamite!"

"Now, what's all this? I don't understand you boys. If I'd known a mere Simmons or two could upset you so much, I'd never have mentioned them. Did you or did you not say there was nothing to worry about?"

"In baseball there's always something to worry about! Anything can happen!"

"Well, never mind. My blood was up. The honor of the McGoniggles was at stake." He gave Mac's sagging shoulders a confident pat. "Don't worry, lad. Just go out there and win one for Uncle Shamus!"

But Mac did worry. "I love Uncle Shamus like a — like an uncle," he said as they pedaled home, "but when it comes to making bets he's a knucklehead! He'd pick a midget to win the high hurdles! I hope this won't be the kiss of death for us!"

"Well, anyway, I'm glad he got a chance to see you in a game, Mac."

"Huh!"

"What's wrong?"

"What isn't? Oh, it was great, and you made a great pitch, and I'm glad we won — but look at me! I finally got behind the plate in a game, and then I never caught a single pitch! Not one!"

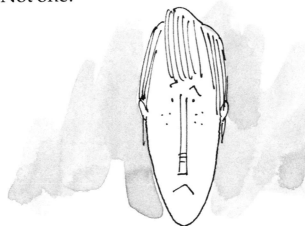

4

THE NEXT GUY that calls me 'One-Pitch Wetzel,' " said Ken, "is going to meet 'One-Punch Wetzel.' "

"I may take some hitting practice myself," said Mac. " 'No-Hit, No-Catch McGoniggle' — I wonder who made that one up?"

"I did," said Ken, "after I heard you'd made up 'One-Pitch Wetzel.' "

Otherwise things were going well. Motty was in winning form on Saturday, but Gunther won their game, too. This left both teams undefeated and ready to settle the championship in the final game at Kilroy High.

"You see, guys?" Chad was confident. "It's like I said!"

"*How* did you spell that?" asked Mac.

"P-U-L-V-E-R-I-Z-E," said Chad.

Ken and Mac went over their Gunther scouting notes again with Coach Coogan, Chad, and Motty.

"That Hawthorne pitcher had a good change-up — it was the only thing Ernie Simmons couldn't hit. But they didn't use it often enough, so he murdered them," said Mac. "Frank, now — the only thing he *did* hit was a change-up. He can't hit fast balls."

"Okay, we'll give Ernie plenty of change-ups," promised Chad.

"And we'll blow Frank down with fast balls," said Motty. "Now, go over the other guys again."

Everyone was feeling good about the big game and ready to go — until Wednesday practice when a foul tip split the thumb on Chad Watson's throwing hand.

"Poor Coach! I think it's worse for him than anyone," said Mac. He and Ken were on their way home. "I wanted to get behind the plate again, but not this way. Without Chad's bat in the lineup, we'll need a miracle!"

"Like twin split thumbs at Gunther?"

When Mac's house came in sight he groaned and hit his bike's brakes.

"Look who's coming down the steps! No, don't look! Turn! Hide me!"

But it was too late. Uncle Shamus had seen them, and was waving.

"You going to tell him, Mac?"

"I guess I'll have to."

"Well, now, lads, I'm glad to see you. I was just telling your mum and dad how proud I am to have a McGoniggle on a winning team, Mac," said Uncle Shamus, shaking hands. "I laughed in Colin Simmons's face last night when he said you were just lucky."

"He said we were lucky, did he?" asked Mac. "I wonder where he got that idea?"

"Of course you're not lucky! You're better than that! So I says to him, 'We'll wait till Saturday to see who's lucky!' I don't mind telling you, my blood was up, and before we finished we doubled our bet, so now it's an even hundred you'll be putting in your uncle's pocket when you press on to a glorious victory. How do you like that for a golden opportunity?"

For a moment Mac looked as if Opportunity had knocked twice, with a sandbag. Then he put a hand on his uncle's shoulder.

"Uncle Shamus, sometimes I wish you'd take something to keep your blood down. We . . . er . . . I — oh, heck, we'll do our best!"

"That you will, and afterward we'll enjoy Colin Simmons's money!"

And with a cheery wave Uncle Shamus strode away briskly down the street.

"You didn't tell him about Chad," said Ken, "and I don't blame you."

Gloom settled like smog over the Kilroy squad. But on Friday . . .

"Chad says he can grip a bat okay! He can hit!"

Hope revived. There was still the question of who should catch, however, since Chad knew he could not handle the constant throwing a catcher has to do.

"Put me on first base again and let Mac catch," he told Coach in a locker-room conference. "He's as good a defensive catcher as I am, he can handle Motty okay."

Mac grinned. "Hey, Motty, stop looking like someone offered you a hot dog instead of a steak!"

"Well, a hot dog is better than an empty plate!" growled Motty.

"Chad is right. That's the best we can do," Coach decided. "But I wonder what else can happen to us?"

A moment later he wished he hadn't asked. The locker-room phone rang.

"Coogan speaking. What? The newspaper's fixed it up to switch the game to Clancy Field?"

Clancy Field was the town ball park, home of the Hamilton City Jaybirds, who were presently on a road trip.

"Now, wait a minute! Yes, I know there's a lot of interest in the game, but . . . Yes, but . . ."

He got nowhere. The principal thought it was a fine idea.

"A certain coach is behind this," Coach fumed as he hung up. "He knows it's an advantage for us to play on our own field!"

But Chad lifted his taped thumb straight up in a victory signal.

"We'll take 'em," he said, "if we have to do it in Yankee Stadium!"

It was an edgy but determined Kilroy team that took the school bus to Clancy Field on Saturday afternoon.

5

KEN STOOD outside the dugout and looked up at the grandstand. "Every seat's filled!"

"Some fuller than others," said Mac. "There's my uncle. And look at the size of the guy with him! That must be Colin Simmons."

The Kilroy infielders were taking their practice grounders from Chad and whipping their throws back to him.

"You'd never know to look at him his thumb still hurts," said Ken admiringly.

Gunther was up first. The game opened badly with a grounder the shortstop fumbled, putting a man on base. But then Motty struck out the next batter and popped up the third man for the second out.

A roar went up from Gunther rooters as their superstar clean-up batter, Ernie Simmons, came to the plate.

Motty's first two pitches were low. Then Ernie fouled one off, and missed a change-up. A knee-high fast ball on the outside caught him looking, with his bat on his shoulder.

"Strike three, you're out!"

"Whaaat?" Ernie jawboned the ump, but of course got nowhere.

"Motty, you've got your stuff today! Your fast ball's jumping!" said Mac on the way to

the dugout, and Motty responded with a gracious, "You're doing okay, too, kid."

In the bottom of the first inning Frank Simmons made his first pitch too good.

"It's a hit! He's going for two! Sliiide —"

"Made it!"

"Look at Frank Simmons!" said Mac. "He's got smoke coming out of his ears!"

Frank was so mad at himself that he missed with his next four pitches, walking the second batter. Ernie trotted out and gave him a talking-to. It was like watching someone talk to himself in the mirror, they were such look-alikes, but the talk got results. The next batter hit a line drive straight at the second baseman.

"Double-play ball!" groaned Ken. "Get— No! He dropped it! Go, go, go!"

Before the ball could be recovered, every-body was safe.

With the bases loaded, Kilroy pandemo-nium broke loose as Chad Watson stepped into the batter's box. He took Frank to three balls and two strikes and then connected for an evening-newspaper headline, no matter who won — SCHOOLBOY HITS ONE OUT OF CLANCY FIELD.

"Nobody out, and four runs ahead!" Mac and Ken pounded each other's backs. "Tell me it's for real, Ken!"

Up in the stands a stunned Colin Simmons was muttering, "Listen, the game isn't over yet . . ."

"Certainly not!" agreed Uncle Shamus. "We're only beginning!"

But Frank Simmons began to show his

stuff. He got the next three batters in order. The game seemed likely to settle into a pitcher's duel, with Gunther trying to play catch-up.

Ernie Simmons led off the fourth with the first hit off Motty. The next batter fouled out, but the third one swung late at a good fast ball and dunked it down the right-field line for a double that brought Ernie home and made the score 4–1. Motty walked the next man, and things looked bad. Mac went to the mound. Chad joined the conference.

"Frank's next after this guy," said Motty. "Maybe we ought to put this guy on and pitch to Frank."

"With only one out?" said Mac. "If we can just get this one, we're in clover — huh, Chad?"

"Right. Come on, Motty, let's get him."

After missing two good pitches, the batter swung again and put up a high foul ball that went toward the Kilroy dugout with Mac right after it, mask off, head cocked back, eyes intent on the ball.

"Catch it, Mac!" yelled Ken as Mac neared the dugout steps.

"Catch him, men!" roared Coach Coogan, who saw himself without a catcher.

The steps and the ball arrived at the same time, with three teammates making grabs for Mac's waist and legs. He ended up almost upside down, but the ball was in his mitt and the umpire's thumb was in the air. As they set him back on his feet Mac grinned his crazy grin.

"I had it all the way!"

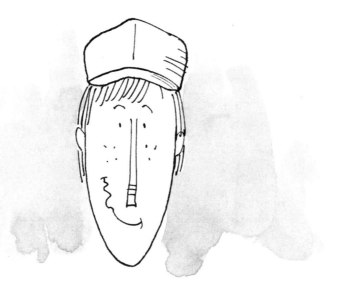

6

AFTER MAC'S GREAT CATCH, Motty fanned Frank Simmons on three straight pitches. The pitcher's duel continued. The game went into the ninth with the score still 4–1, Kilroy.

Gunther's scheduled hitters in the ninth were the second and third batters and the clean-up man, Ernie Simmons. From the dugout the Kilroy bench warmers did their best as bench jockeys.

"Keep it coming, Motty! Keep it coming!"

"Blow 'em down!"

Just three more outs and the game was in the books! One nervous bench warmer started pacing back and forth in the runway that led to the dressing room.

"Stop walking around back there!" bawled their jumpy leader.

"I can't watch, Coach!"

"If I can, you can!"

"Okay, okay!" said Ken.

The first batter worked the count to three and two.

"Don't walk him!" moaned Ken.

"Take your hand off your eyes, Wetzel!"

"I'm peeking through my fingers, Coach!"

"Strike three!" bellowed the umpire.

The next batter hit a long fly to left field, but not long enough. Two outs! Everyone on the

team could think of only one thing now —
what a perfect finish if Motty could nail Ernie
Simmons for the final out. Nobody was sit-
ting down, anywhere in the park. Mac trotted
to the mound with the ball. Chad came over
from first base.

"One more, Motty!"

"Let's get him and go home!"

"I took him the first time and I'll do it
again!"

"Right, Motty! We'll give him some change-ups, and —"

"No, he'll be looking for them. I'll get him with low hard ones on the outside, like before."

"Mac may be right, though —" began Chad.

"Don't worry, guys! I've got my stuff!"

"Well . . . be careful!" said Mac.

Ernie dug in ferociously in the right-hand batter's box — big, hard-eyed, dangerous. Motty burned one in.

BAM!

Ernie didn't hit one out of the park, but he hit one so far over the centerfielder's head he could have tap-danced around the bases twirling a cane before the ball got back.

Uproar in the stands. Groans in the Kilroy

dugout. Another conference on the mound, with Motty kicking dirt in all directions.

"I blew it! Why didn't I listen!"

"Never mind, forget it, we've still got the game. This next guy — Garcia — that's all that matters."

In the dugout Coach Coogan was hurting.

"I can't watch!" he snapped, and then corrected himself. "Yes, I can! If Ken can, I can!"

But Garcia hit one to right center for a triple, at which point Coach turned to Ken. "Start warming up!"

Ken and Tommy took off for the bullpen, breathing hard.

When things go bad in a ball game they seem to go all the way. The next batter had hardly touched the ball in four trips to the plate, but now —

"Oh, no! Grab it! Throw to home!" Mac was shouting, but the ball got past everyone — one of those miserable little infield hits no one could handle — and Garcia was home with a run that made it 4–3.

While Ken threw harder and harder in the bullpen, Motty came apart at the seams. He walked the next two batters, and the bases were loaded. The only good thing anyone could think of was that Gunther's next scheduled batter was Frank Simmons.

By now Ken and Tommy had stopped to watch the game.

"Frank's up next. Now Gunther's in a pickle!" said Tommy, determined to find a ray of hope. "If they pinch-hit for Frank they'll have to use their second-string pitcher against us in the bottom of the ninth. But it's now or never, so they'll *have* to pinch-hit."

"Motty's just *got* to settle down, that's all!"

Coach Coogan came out of the dugout, raised his hand, and jerked his thumb. Ken felt as if his cap were spinning on his head.

"Let's go, Ken!" said Tommy. "You're in!"

7

WITH A SET FACE, Motty was striding off
toward the dugout, getting a big hand. Gulp-
ing, Ken hitched up his pants and did his best
to simulate a confident stroll to the mound.
Mac and Chad were waiting for him.

"Mac says you can handle this guy," said
Chad. "Go to it!"

"You mean Frank?" Ken gave Mac a
panic-stricken look. "But what if they pinch-
hit for him?"

Mac's nutty eyes glittered.

"Let 'em. You're going to hold this, no matter *who* comes to bat!"

By then, however, Ken wasn't listening. He was staring over Mac's shoulder, and so was Chad.

"Well, look who's coming! Old Number One," said Chad, that being the modest number Frank Simmons wore. "I guess they figure Frank can hit a second-string pitcher. Well, show them, Ken! Just blow him down, and we'll all go home!"

"Happy days! Give him smoke," said Mac. "No change-ups!"

It helped Ken to watch Frank step into the lefties' batter's box and know he was facing a weak hitter. If only he could repeat his first relief appearance! Another liner to Chad — anything! Anything but a hit, and runners streaming across the plate!

His first pitch, hard and on the inside, got a feeble wave that missed by a mile. Confidence surged through Ken. He was going to do it!

His next pitch was nearer the center of the plate. Too near.

Smack!

The ball ripped down the line over the third baseman's head, curving, and landed far out in left field —

About two inches over the foul line.

It was only a long foul ball, but during those

few seconds Ken had died a little. Even a weak hitter connected sometimes if you gave him a fat pitch. Mac came galloping out, looking as angry as Ken had ever seen him.

"I know, I know, it was a dumb pitch!" said Ken. "I almost blew the game."

"What do you mean? *I* almost blew it!"

When Mac told him what he meant, and what he wanted Ken to do next, Ken had heard everything.

"You sure?"

"You bet I'm sure!"

Mac walked back to the plate. Ken stood kneading the ball with trembling hands. The noise from the stands was deafening, but he scarcely heard it. He had worked hard on the pitch; it was a good one; but this time it had to be the best he'd ever thrown.

He set himself, blew out his breath, took a look at the runner on third, went into his stretch, and threw.

It was a beauty of a change-up, just enough taken off its speed but not too much, and it was on target. He saw the batter, set for a fast ball, blink and hesitate, and finally swing —

Plop!

"Strike three, you're out!"

The instant the ball was in his mitt Mac came to his feet. Under the roar from the stands he shouted in the batter's ear:

"Next time don't just trade shirts — trade shoes, too — Ernie!"

Coach Coogan glanced around the select group he had gathered together — Chad, Motty, Ken, and Mac.

"For the good of the game, and because we could never prove it anyway, we're gonna keep this quiet, but I figured you two guys have a right to know the facts," he said, nodding at Chad and Motty. "Go ahead, Mac."

The Great McGoniggle obliged. "Well, I don't have to tell you, Chad, that when a catcher is down behind the plate he sees a lot of shoes. Now, I happened to notice that Frank's heels were dirty from kicking holes in the mound before he started pitching, but suddenly, in that last inning, when he creamed that shot down the foul line, an alarm went off in my head. Because now Frank's *toes* were dirty, as if he'd been balancing on them behind the plate, and his heels were clean!

"Right then I knew that Ernie was a switch-hitter. He can hit both left and right. Maybe Frank can, too, but either way Ernie's probably ten times as good a hitter.

"They'd slipped down the runway to their dressing room and swapped shirts, and they could easily have gone back between innings and swapped again.

"So here was Ernie pretending to be Frank, and never for one minute expecting a change-up."

"Beautiful, beautiful!" crowed Coach Coogan, reliving the glorious moment. But then his eyes narrowed. "Don't think, though, I ain't gonna enjoy letting a certain coach know that *we* know! And by the way, Mac — how did your uncle like it?"

"Well, he insisted on splitting with me, so then I talked him into betting his fifty against my fifty — I bet him he couldn't stop betting for six months."

"What? He actually took the bet?"

"He couldn't help himself. By the time I got through with him, his blood was up!"